W9-CLW-004

...res and often tells stories, all of it magic and all of it true.

...es and all of the stories, and all of the magic, the music is you.

— John Denver —

Guest Dedication by John Denver's Daughter

Please enjoy this beautiful book! Here's to the dolphins in these pages, in our d
future. And here's to my dad, who loved the ocean enough to sing about it. — A

Dedication by the Illustrator
For Crit Warren — mentor, friend and creative inspirer.
— C.C.

Acknowledgements by the Publisher
Many thanks to children's literary agent Sandy Ferguson Fuller of Alp Arts Company, who wh
alive conceived the idea of bringing John's spirit to children through children's books, and after
it to fruition; also to Hal Thau, John's long-time friend and business manager; Jim Bell of Bell L
Connelly and Keith Hauprich of Cherry Lane Music Publishing Company.

"Ancient Rhymes" Words and Music by John Denver
and Bob Samples. Copyright **(c)** 1991 Cherry
Mountain Music (ASCAP)/Dream Works
Songs (ASCAP). Worldwide rights for
Cherry Mountain Music and Dream
Works Songs administered by Cherry
Lane Music Publishing Company, Inc.
(ASCAP) All Rights Reserved.
Used By Permission.

"The Music Is You"
Copyright ©
Cor
assig
Zad

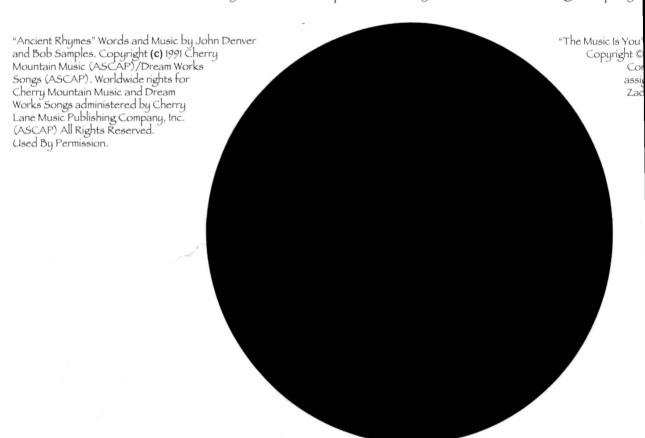

A Sharing Nature With Children Book
Copyright © 2004 Dawn Publications · Illustrations © 2004 Christopher Canyon · All rights res
Dawn Publications · 12402 Bitney Springs Road · Nevada City, California 95959 · www.dawnpub.

Library of Congress Cataloging-in-Publication Data
Canyon, Christopher
John Denver's Ancient Rhymes: a dolphin lullaby/adapted & illustrated by Christopher Canyon.
p. cm.
"A Sharing Nature With Children Book."
Summary: A picture book adaptation of John Denver's song Ancient Rhymes, celebrating the birth o
ISBN 1-58469-064-X (hardback with attached cd)--ISBN 1-58469-065-8 (pbk)
1. Children's songs--Texts. [1. Dolphins--Songs and music. 2. Songs.] 1. Title: Ancient Rhymes. II. Denver,
PZ8.3.C1925 J1 2004
782.42164'0268--dc22   2004004414

Book Design & Production by Christopher Canyon
Printed in China
10 9 8 7 6 5 4 3 2 1
First Edition

John Denver's

Ancient Rhymes
A Dolphin Lullaby

Adapted & Illustrated by
Christopher Canyon

DAWN PUBLICATIONS

Two days before the moon was round,

You felt the urge

of sun's light beams.

The muffled world of dolphin sound,

slipped down and back into your dreams.

For nine full months that passed before,

you learned of all of life's ancient rhymes,

Then mother sensed a farther shore,

and brought you forth

into these times.

So taste the air of your new world

and gently guide us to your mind.

It knows the wind

and sails unfurled,

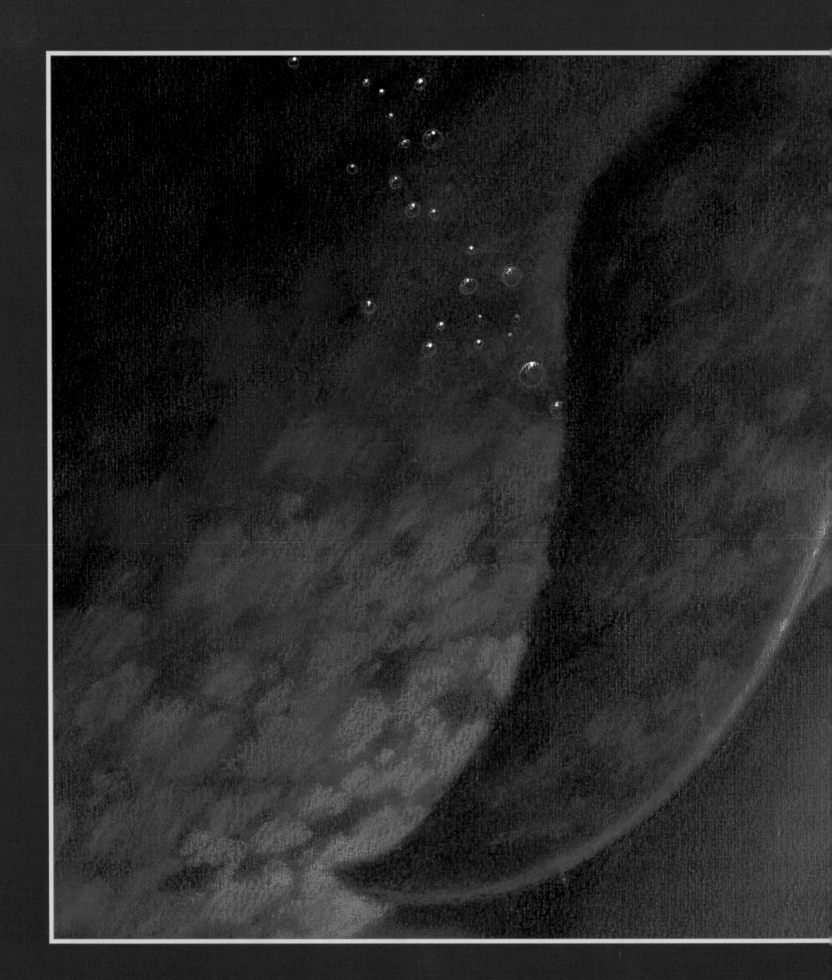

and holds to heart, the dolphin kind.

Welcome precious earth-made child,

we met you first in your father's songs

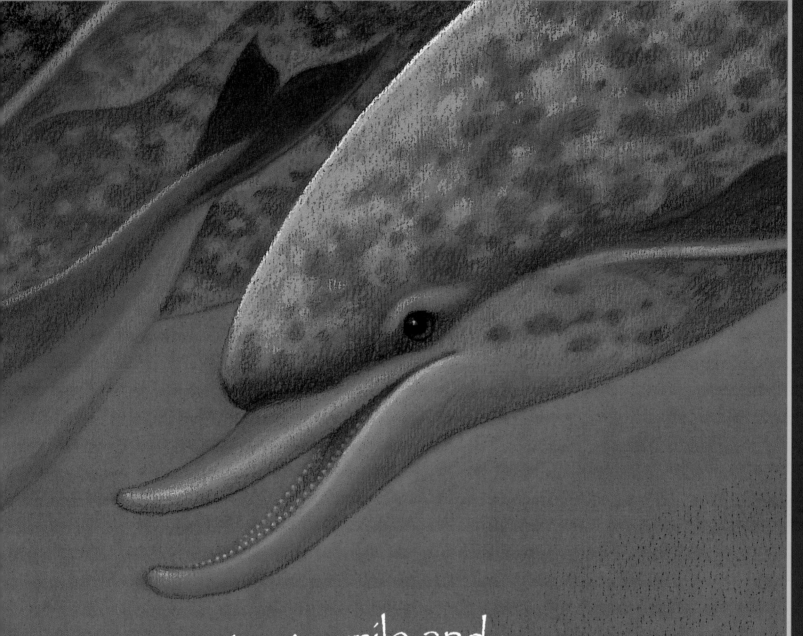

and mother's smile and waters wild,

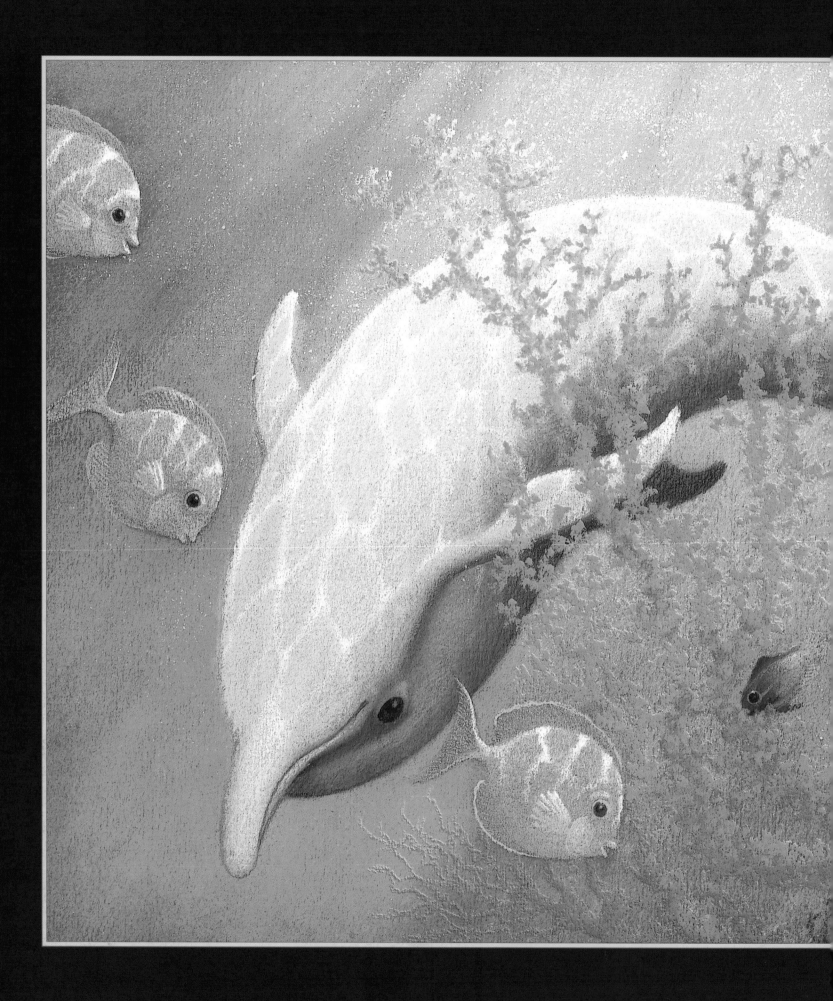

it's in this place you now belong.

I know you know of all these things,

and feel the faith of a dolphin's sigh,

For you were born on silver wings

to taste the high blown crystal sky.

So sing one day to all of us

the songs you learned in dolphin lair.

Giving hope to life as all we must,

and teach us how their grace to share.

John Denver loved dolphins. He put on a snorkel mask and swam with them. He put on scuba equipment and dove with them. Their grace ... their power ... their curiosity ... their songs. Their eyes, like those of a bright child, were windows into another world. He felt them seeming to communicate with him. He and his wife Cassandra, while she was seven months pregnant, swam closely with a female dolphin, and Cassandra "felt her communicate with me and the baby inside of me." This song was written during that time, in 1991. For John it was a magical experience. He could hardly get enough.

Photo courtesy of Lowell Norman

John loved to be in the water, and particularly to be around dolphins.

Dolphins are highly intelligent creatures with strong social bonds and a complex language of their own. They suckle their young. They often touch, rub and caress each other, and "dance" with swirling grace. Wistfully, we humans think that someday dolphins may talk to us, and we to them.

John's feelings came though his music, and reverberated in hearts everywhere, making him one of the top selling vocal artists of all time. Over 32 million John Denver albums have sold in the United States alone. Yet John Denver was much more than an entertainer. He believed that everyone can make a difference, and he put his own feelings into action. He actively supported The Cousteau Society's campaign to protect the marine habitat (www.cousteausociety.org). He supported the Human/Dolphin Foundation. He co-founded the Hunger Project, which is committed to ending world hunger forever (www.thp.org). He created Plant-It 2000, now renamed Plant-It 2020, an organization that has already planted one million trees (www.plantit2020.org). He bought nearly 1000 acres of spectacular Colorado land and gave it to the Windstar Foundation (www.wstar.org) to carry on environmental education. And he kept singing and writing songs until his death in 1997 when a small experimental plane he was soloing (John loved to fly!) crashed into the Pacific Ocean. The John Denver & Kids Book Series is dedicated to bringing this spirit to children.

Throughout his life Christopher Canyon has been deeply touched by John Denver's music. "John's songs have always given me hope, joy and an unbounded belief in possibilities," he says. Christopher is an award winning artist, musician and performer. His time is divided between illustrating children's books and presenting at schools and conferences. As a popular speaker and performer, one of his favorite messages is that everyone has what it takes to be artistic. "As humans we are all creative beings. If we celebrate and use our creativity in a positive way it's amazing how much we can learn and how much joy we have to share."

Ancient Rhymes is the eighth book Christopher Canyon has illustrated for Dawn Publications. To learn more about him, please visit the "Authors & Illustrators" section on Dawn Publications' website, www.dawnpub.com. He lives in historic German Village in Columbus, Ohio where he, his wife Jeanette Canyon—also a children's book artist—and their three feline family members create picture books for children.

Dawn Publications is dedicated to inspiring in children a deeper understanding and appreciation for all life on Earth. Some titles present particular animals, habitats or aspects of nature; others focus on more universal qualities. In each case, our purpose is to encourage a life-long bond with the natural world. For our catalog go to www.dawnpub.com, or call 800-545-7475.

Ancient Rhymes
A Dolphin Lullaby

Words and Music by
John Denver and Bob Samples